THE SHOEMAKER'S GIFT

FROM AN ANCIENT CHINESE FOLKTALE — INTERPRETED & ILLUSTRATED BY LYNDELL LUDWIG

ISBN 0-916870-53-7
Library of Congress Catalog No. 82-73196.

Creative Arts Book Company
833 Bancroft Way
Berkeley, California 94710

CREATIVE ARTS BOOKS
ARE PUBLISHED BY
DONALD S. ELLIS

To Ch'eh Tsu-ying
wherever you are.

Many years ago, far away in a village
in China, there lived a shoemaker. The
shoemaker was especially skilled at making
sandals and other footwear for the people in
the village. He was poor, but he liked what
he did and he worked very hard at his craft.

One day the shoemaker came in
possession of an unusual piece of leather.

"Ah! What a fine piece of leather," he
thought to himself. "It is not often I see a hide such
as this one. I will make a pair of hunting boots out of it."

1

With that the shoemaker set to

work. He knew just how he wanted the boots to

look. He started designing them by making a pattern

from an old piece of rice paper. When the pattern was ready

he laid it out on the leather. Carefully, he cut the leather along the lines of

the pattern and fitted the pieces together. Then the fashioning of the boots began in earnest.

The shoemaker worked hard on the boots, using every bit of skill and knowledge he had. He worked in his spare

time and often far into the quiet hours of the night. So engrossed was he in the task
that he barely knew when the sun rose or set.

Finally the boots were finished. The shoemaker polished the boots and buffed them.
Then he set them on a shelf in the little shop which stretched across the front part of his
house. Outside, the moon and the stars shone brightly and an owl hooted through the
night air. But the shoemaker noticed none of this. He was too tired. He was also very
happy and pleased with what he had done. As soon as he put the boots on the shelf,
he climbed into bed and fell asleep.

At daybreak the shoemaker's wife got up as usual to prepare the morning meal. She knew how hard her husband had been working and when she saw he was still asleep she tiptoed about so as not to waken him.

Then she saw the finished boots sitting on the shelf. They were strong and handsomely made. There was not a flaw in the workmanship anywhere. And they were pleasing to look at. "What an unusually handsome pair of boots," exclaimed the shoemaker's wife to herself and she smiled broadly.

4

Soon the shoemaker
woke up. He joined his wife and they both
looked at the boots and marveled at their beauty. During the
day customers came into the little shop. They saw the boots
on the shelf. Each one stopped to admire them. Word spread
throughout the village and, as the day wore on, more and more people
began to drop by especially to see the boots. Everyone gazed at the boots and praised
the shoemaker for making as splendid a pair of hunting boots as any of them had ever seen.

Night fell. Finally the last person left the shop and the shoemaker and his wife were alone. The
shoemaker's wife picked up one of the boots and turned it over in her hands. "You know," she said. "It
really would be a shame to sell these boots to just anyone."

5

Her eyes twinkled. Then she looked at her husband. "You must take the boots and present them to the king!" she said suddenly in a clear voice.

The shoemaker stared at his wife in amazement. Then he looked at the boots. Truly these boots were unusually handsome. And they were skillfully crafted as well. And he did not feel this way just because he had made them. Indeed, they were fit for a king.

"All right!" he said. "I will do just that! I will take the boots and present them to the king."

The next day, the shoemaker arose early from his bed and ate his morning meal. While he did this, his wife wrapped the boots carefully in a fine piece of silk cloth. She also tucked a few rice cakes into her husband's coat for him to eat along the way. When all was ready, the shoemaker slung the boots over his shoulder and said goodbye to his wife. Then he started out toward the city where the king lived.

The city was several hours distant by foot.
It was surrounded by a high wall
to keep out invading tribes and roving bandits.
You could see the wall of the city from miles away
throughout the countryside.

The shoemaker approached the main gate to the city. When the sentry who guarded the gate

saw the shoemaker, he stood at attention and blocked the shoemaker's way with his spear.

"Halt!" said the sentry to the shoemaker. "What do you want?" he asked sharply. "State your

business or I cannot let you enter the city!"

The shoemaker looked at the sentry. "I have brought a present to give to the king," he replied.

9

The sentry looked at the bundle the shoemaker carried on his shoulder. Then he relaxed a little and lowered his voice. "When anyone gives the king a present," he said, "the king always grants him something in return. If you will agree to give me one-third of whatever the king offers you, I will then let you go through the gate and into the city."

The shoemaker was puzzled. Somehow this did not seem quite right to him. But after a pause he agreed to the sentry's request and the sentry immediately let him enter the city.

The shoemaker walked through the city streets and headed toward the palace. A second sentry stood on guard at the entrance to the palace grounds. When the shoemaker approached the entrance, the sentry stepped in front of him and blocked his way.

"Halt!" he said in a firm voice. "What do you want? State your business or I cannot let you enter the palace!"

"I want to see the king," replied the shoemaker. "I have a present to give him."

"Oh!" said the sentry. Then he lowered his voice and leaned forward. "Everybody who comes to the palace entrance wants to see the king. But I'll tell you what I will do. If you agree to give me one-third of whatever the king bestows on you in return for the present, I will let you enter the palace grounds."

"Ai!" thought the shoemaker to himself. "Everyone here is a swindler! All I want to do is to give the king a pair of boots." Then he said aloud, "All right, I agree to give you one-third of whatever the king bestows on me." Immediately, the sentry stepped aside and let the shoemaker enter the palace grounds. The shoemaker walked across the courtyard and into the main hall. Just inside the portals of the main hall were two great doors. A third sentry guarded the doors. The sentry stepped forward and raised his arm.

"Halt!" he said to the shoemaker in a loud voice. "State your business or I cannot let you into the king's chambers."

"I have come to give the king a present," the shoemaker replied in a clear, steady voice.

"I see," said the sentry as he looked at the bundle the shoemaker carried over his shoulder. Then he lowered his voice to almost a whisper. "Not everyone can pass through these doors to see the king," he said. "However, if you will promise to give me one-third of whatever the king gives you, I will be happy to open the doors and let you go in."

This time, the shoemaker replied to the sentry without hesitation. "I promise to give you one-third of whatever the king gives me," he said. At once the sentry turned and pulled open the two great doors.

13

The shoemaker took a deep breath and bowed his head. Then he walked over the threshold and entered the king's chambers.

The king sat on a raised platform at the far end of the long chamber room. Two servants stood in back of him slowly waving fans on long poles.

The shoemaker faced the king and the two great doors closed behind him. The king motioned for him to come closer. The shoemaker walked down the long hall to the foot of the broad steps leading to the platform on which the king sat. He took the bundle from his shoulder and put it down on the floor. Then he knelt and bowed his head three times.

"Who are you?" the king asked the shoemaker. "What do you want?"

"I am a village shoemaker," the shoemaker replied with his hands together and his head still bowed. "Not long ago I came in possession of a fine piece of leather. I made the leather into a pair of hunting boots. Everyone in the village where I live came to see the boots. They all admired them. After they had gone, my wife said the boots were so splendid they were worthy only for a king to wear. We both agreed. Therefore I have brought them here to give to you.

15

The king leaned forward. He watched the shoemaker open the bundle and display the hunting boots. They were truly beautiful. The king stood up and walked down from the platform. He picked up the boots to have a look at them. He turned the boots over and over in his hands. "Aaaa!" he said. "These are indeed an unusually fine looking pair of boots. I can see that the craftsmanship is of the highest order. You are to be commended for your skill and ability."

Then the king sat right down on the lower step and tried the boots on. They were not too big and not too small. In fact, they were a perfect fit. The king stood up. He walked back up on the platform. He lifted his robes a little and

looked at the
boots on his feet. Then he
smiled at the shoemaker.

"I gratefully accept these
hunting boots," he said.
"And, since it is the imperial
custom, it is now my pleasure to bestow upon
you a gift in appreciation. If it is within my power I will grant whatever you may wish."

The shoemaker looked thoughtful. Then he said, "Oh honorable king, I did not come here to receive a gift from
you. Whatever pleasure the boots may bring you is reward enough for me. However, if it is an imperial custom, and
it so please your majesty, I do have one request. Would you, great king, issue an order that one of your strongest
guards give me ninety-nine blows with a long hard wooden stick?"

17

The king was astonished. He looked at the shoemaker closely. "What?" he asked.

"You want me to issue an order that one of my strongest guards give you ninety-nine blows with a long hard wooden stick? Surely you must want something better than this!"

"No!" the shoemaker replied earnestly. "My only wish is that you fulfill this request."

"This is truly an unusual request," the king said, half to himself. He looked at the shoemaker out of the corner of his eyes. "However, when a man is so determined that he cannot be persuaded otherwise, who am I not to grant his request?"

18

With that, the king turned to his chief secretary. "I hereby order that this shoemaker receive ninety-nine blows with a long hard wooden stick," he said. "The blows are to be delivered by the strongest of the royal guard."

Then he added, "But tell the guard to be careful he doesn't strike too hard lest the shoemaker be hurt."

"Don't be too careful!" the shoemaker spoke up in a loud voice. "Tell the guard to strike as hard as he can. In fact, the harder the blows the better," he added, half smiling.

All this was very puzzling to the king. But he let the order stand, and the chief secretary issued the command for the preparations to be made.

Then the chief secretary led the shoemaker out of the palace, through the city, and out the city gate to the place where the blows were to be delivered.

19

The third sentry who let the shoemaker enter the king's chambers was still on duty outside the two great doors of the chamber room. The shoemaker leaned toward the sentry as he passed him. "Follow me," he whispered, "and I will see that you receive your one-third portion of the king's gift."

The third sentry motioned to an alternate sentry nearby. The alternate stepped forward and took over the post by the two great doors while the third sentry fell in step behind the shoemaker and the chief secretary.

At the palace entrance the second sentry stood at attention. As the shoemaker passed the sentry he bent toward him. "Follow me," he whispered, "and I will see that you receive one-third of what the king has given me, just as I promised I would."

The second sentry motioned for an alternate to take his place at the palace entrance. Then he followed quickly along behind the third sentry, the shoemaker, and the chief secretary.

When they reached the main gate to the city, the first sentry stood guard outside with his head held high and his eyes facing straight ahead. The shoemaker walked directly in front of him. As he did so he whispered to the sentry.

"Follow me and I will see that you receive your one-third portion of the gift the king has granted me," he said.

Immediately the first sentry beckoned to a fellow sentry. The fellow sentry came over at once to stand guard at the gate in his place. Then the first sentry hurried along behind the second and third sentries, and the shoemaker and the chief secretary.

The little group walked a short distance from the city gate to a
level place where a bench had already been set up. Beside the bench
stood two strong guards. One of the guards held a long hard wooden
stick in his hands.

As soon as the group reached the bench, the king's chief secretary
prepared to state the king's order and see that it was faithfully carried
out. Personally he was a little more than curious to know why the
shoemaker made the request for the ninety-nine blows.

The king's chief secretary stood ready to speak. He looked at the
shoemaker. Before he could say anything the shoemaker spoke up.

"Now," said the shoemaker to the secretary. "Here is how matters
stand. Today I came to the city to give the king a present. Before I could see the king
I had to pass by these three sentries standing beside us. In turn each sentry said he would
only let me pass his post if I would agree to give him one-third of whatever the king granted me in return
for the present I had brought for him, as was the imperial custom. The king has granted me ninety-nine blows
with a long hard wooden stick. To fulfill my promises to these three sentries, I now ask that the king's order be carried

out and that the guard with the long hard wooden stick strike each of the sentries one-third of the ninety-nine blows."

"Ho ho! So this is how it is!" said the chief secretary, and he chuckled to himself.

Then the secretary stepped forward and turned and faced the three sentries. He raised his hand and spoke in a loud commanding voice.

23

"By order of his imperial majesty, the king, I hereby decree that each of you three sentries shall receive thirty-three blows. This decree is to be carried out immediately. And don't be too careful how hard you strike them," he added to the guard who held the stick. "The king's order says the harder the blows the better."

24

By this time a crowd had gathered.

The guard who held the long hard wooden stick rolled up his sleeves. The second guard instructed the sentry whose post was at the main gate of the city to lean over the bench. The guard with the stick administered thirty-three blows on the sentry's back. When he finished, the sentry whose post was just outside the palace entrance was ushered forward. He, too, leaned over the bench and received his third of the ninety-nine blows. Lastly the sentry who stood watch outside the two great doors of the king's chambers stepped up, and the guard struck him the thirty-three blows which were his portion.

25

While the imperial decree was being carried out, word spread among the people who had gathered to see what was happening. By the time the ninety-nine blows had been delivered, the people knew all about the hunting boots and the shoemaker and the three sentries who had demanded a bribe from him. As the last sentry received his final blow, the people all shouted and cheered.

"Long live the impartial shoemaker!" they cried out. "He has justly repaid those who tried to cheat him." And they shook the shoemaker's hands and smiled at him in admiration.

The king, still inside his chambers, heard the people shouting and cheering outside the city. "What is that noise?" he asked. "Who is making such an uproar outside the city gates?" Immediately the king strode out of the palace and up the steps of the stone wall that surrounded the city. He walked to the watchtower atop the main gate of the wall and looked down at the assembled crowd. At the edge of the crowd he saw his chief secretary nodding his head and smiling at the shoemaker.

28

The king sent a messenger to fetch the chief secretary. The secretary hurried at once to

the watchtower. He told the king all about the three sentries and how they had tried to cheat the shoemaker.

The king's eyes sparkled and he began to laugh. "No wonder the shoemaker made such an unsual request," he said. "And no wonder he wanted the guard to strike the blows so hard."

The king ordered the shoemaker to be brought before him. When the shoemaker arrived at the watchtower the king patted him on the shoulder. "You did exactly the right thing," he said.   29

The shoemaker smiled at the king. Then he folded his arms, bowed three times, and slowly backed away to make his exit.

Since everyone leaving the king's presence must keep his eyes lowered to the ground, the last thing the shoemaker saw of the king was the beautiful pair of hunting boots he had fashioned with his own hands, for the king was still wearing them.

And that night after the shoemaker returned to his home in the village he slept soundly and well in his bed.

Toward the end of World War I, Lyndell Ludwig's father taught at Nan Kai University in Tientsin, China, and returned with a love for the Chinese people and culture. Exposed to things Chinese from her earliest years, Lyndell soon developed similar interests. She went on to major in Far Eastern studies at the University of Washington and at Berkeley, and discovered a wealth of children's stories, most of them never translated from the Chinese. Applying her artistic talents, she set out to bring these delightful tales to the West.

Lyndell, who lives in Berkeley, California, continues to find Chinese stories that beg to be retold.